18

With much love to Alastair and
Stella. Jings! Ye're an affy braw pair
C.S.

For Kaspar
S.B

First published in 2014 by
Scholastic Children's Books,
Euston House, 24 Eversholt Street
London NW1 1DB a division of Scholastic Ltd
www.scholastic.co.uk
London ~ New York ~ Toronto ~ Sydney ~ Auckland
Mexico City ~ New Delhi ~ Hong Kong

Text copyright © 2014 Chae Strathie
Illustrations copyright © 2014 Sebastien Braun

PB ISBN 978 1407 13818 3

Bedtime for Tiny Mouse

Written by Chae Strathie

Illustrated by Sebastien Braun

■SCHOLASTIC

Tiny Mouse couldn't sleep.

He curled and twirled . . .

flipped and flopped . . .

snuggled and huggled . . .

But he was still wide awake.

So he climbed out of bed and scampered off to the living room.

"Mummy Mouse," he sighed, "I can't sleep a wink. My head's full of fizz and my eyes won't stay shut."

"Try counting sheep," said Mummy Mouse.
"That will send you to sleep."

Tiny Mouse scurried back to his bedroom and began counting sheep in his head.

At first the sheep jumped nicely.
But then they started doing cartwheels,
star jumps and ridiculous roly-polies.

Tiny Mouse
couldn't keep up!

So he climbed out of bed and padded off to the kitchen.

"Daddy Mouse," he sighed, "I can't sleep a wink. My feet are full of fireworks and my knees won't behave."

"Try drinking this cup of warm milk," said Daddy Mouse. "That will send you to sleep."

Tiny Mouse trotted back to his bedroom and sipped his milk.

He soon began
to feel drowsy.
But then a drop of milk
dribbled down his nose.

"AAAA-CHOO!"

He sneezed so hard, he fell right out of bed!

So he hopped off to see his big brother Milo.
"Milo!" he shouted, "I can't sleep a wink.
My tail is twitchy and my ears are excited."

Milo was listening to his favourite loud music. "Try dancing round your room to tire yourself out," said Milo. "That will send you to sleep."

Tiny Mouse hurried back to his bedroom and started dancing.

Round and round he went, jigging faster and faster.

He tried ballet . . .

he tried hip-hop . . .

he even did the Highland Fling.

But nothing tired him
out. He was more
awake than ever.

So he skipped to the front porch.

"Grandma Mouse," he sighed, "I can't sleep."

"Is your head full of fizz?" asked Grandma Mouse.

"Yes," sighed Tiny Mouse.

"And are your feet full of fireworks?"

"Yes," said Tiny Mouse. "Even my whiskers
are wide awake."

Grandma Mouse looked up at the deep, dark sky where a golden moon floated peacefully.

"I know just what to do," she said.

Grandma patted her knee and Tiny
Mouse scrambled up.
   "The Mouse in the Moon will sing
you to sleep," said Grandma.

"But he's very shy, so first
you must close your eyes."

Tiny Mouse shut his eyes and by
and by a soft voice began singing.

"Lay down your head,
Little dreamer,
Close sleepy eyes.

Time to drift off,
Little dreamer,
Beneath starry skies.

Cosy and warm,
Little dreamer,
Arms hold you tight.

Sleep safe and sound,
Little dreamer,
All through the night."

Tiny Mouse felt very sleepy. The fireworks in his feet flew away and the fizz fizzled out of his head. His frisky whiskers drooped and his knees settled down at last.

Grandma Mouse carefully carried him indoors and tucked him up in bed.

Tiny Mouse
curled and
twirled . . .

flipped and flopped . . .

snuggled and huggled . . .

...and finally fell fast asleep.

"Goodnight, little dreamer," whispered Grandma Mouse.

"Sleep tight."

The End